CHERRY BLOSSOM EYES

S.T. CARTLEDGE

ERASERHEAD PRESS
PORTLAND, OREGON

ERASERHEAD PRESS
P.O. BOX 10065
PORTLAND, OR 97296

www.eraserheadpress.com
facebook/eraserheadpress

ISBN: 978-1-62105-267-8
Copyright © 2019 by S.T. Cartledge
Cover design copyright © 2019 by Hauke Vagt

Printed in the USA.

PART ONE

SEASON OF THE COLD

The sun came up a cherry blossom and burst its rose gold light into the sky. Its scent was pure and fresh, its petals flickered playfully in the cosmic wind and cast the light dancing down upon the Isle of Flowers.

The flowers which grew here were cherry blossoms, little versions of our glorious sun, and each one glowed as little beacons and died with the season of the Cold.

Margot and I were sitting cliffside on this morning after spending the night watching the cherry blossom trees shed their glowing flowers, sending them drifting out into the slick black ocean before winking out forever.

"And so the ocean swallows the light," Margot said.

"And so the Cold begins," I replied.

The cherry blossom sun had a warmth and kindness to it which couldn't be denied, and yet the first day of Cold already made itself known with brittle fingers, brittle bones.

If our limbs were branches they would surely snap and become another offering to the ocean.

We could see down at the beach the first bonfires were being built. When we were little human seedlings, Margot and I would come down to the beach on the first day of Cold with our parents and watch the lighting of the bonfires. The dead trees became offerings for the sky. The heat became the comfort fuel which carried us through the Cold. The bonfires burned throughout the Cold and we would all take turns tending them, making sure they would not go out.

"The bonfires look like they're going to be smaller again this year," Margot observed.

"Much smaller," I replied.

"Might not make it through the Cold," she said.

"Might not," I agreed.

Each year we held the same conversations, shared our doubts with each other, knew that each year became harder than the last.

We the people of the Isle of Flowers collectively started harvesting cherry blossom seeds and collectively planted them each year in the season of the Birth, to sprout the tree seedlings to replace the ones which died for good.

The seeds we planted grew in number each year, but we just had to look to know it was not enough. The season of the Blossom bore less flowers and less each year while we could do nothing but dig our hands into the soil with the seeds of the trees and give them fresh water from the mountain stream and hope over time they will sprout and glow and live forever like the sun.

We knew they wouldn't live forever but we wished it all the same.

The season of the Cold was tough and unforgiving, but it was also the best season of the three.

BONFIRE DAY

Down on the beach we felt the fine white sand squeak beneath bare feet. The ocean waves crashed upon the beach. The foam was ice cold. There were hundreds of barefoot people on the beach, most of them coming and going with trunks and branches, chopping wood for the remaining bonfires being built. The work wrapped all around the coast, and up from the beach there were more people working, bringing truckloads of dead cherry blossom trees down from the town and from the cherry blossom forest from the other side of town.

We found the foreman walking up and down the beach, barking orders to the people, making sure the bonfires were built correctly so they would burn bright enough to keep us warm and burn bright enough so they could ward off the tourists until the season of the Blossom.

"How many bonfires this year?" Margot asked the foreman.

"Thirteen," he replied. He yelled at the group of people at the nearest bonfire to undo what they just did and replace the timber a certain way.

"That's three less than last year," Margot said.

"A lot less timber than last year," he said. He yelled at the group to do the thing again.

Someone in the group yelled back in frustration.

The foreman sighed and turned to Margot, "are you two any good at building bonfires?"

She paused before answering. Enough time for the waves to crash and recede. "We've seen it done enough I think we could manage."

"Alright you lot," he called out to the bonfire builders. "Leave this stack and get to collecting and chopping."

The group dropped their timber in the sand and scurried up the beach. I had a feeling they might not bother collecting or chopping wood, but instead just keep on walking right back into town. I didn't think the foreman would care either way. He left Margot and myself to work on building the bonfire on our own and disappeared up the beach.

The thing about the first day of Cold is that if we don't get these bonfires built and lit by sundown we're in for a freezing night, and lighting the bonfires the next day becomes near on impossible. No wonder the foreman was always on edge.

We called it Bonfire Day.

We got the heart of the bonfire built without any harassment from the foreman. A sigh of relief, as our hands were sore and covered in splinters, and time was our enemy. The other bonfires were being built in teams rotating out throughout the day, but the foreman more-or-less left Margot and myself to our own devices, only sending people our way to drop more timber.

Once the heart of the bonfire was done the hammers and nails were passed around to all the builders. The hammers gripped and squeezed the splinters deep into our tender hands. A big bucket of nails was dropped at the base of our bonfire. A ladder was brought to us along with large planks of timber to start shaping the bonfire into its final form.

We anchored the largest bits of timber into the ground around the heart and nailed the other pieces around it to form a skeleton to protect it against the ocean and the wind. The shapes of the branches were odd and varied, chopped up bits to loosely form its shape. Over hours of hammering nails into wood, the skeleton reached its many twisted arms toward the sky

Once when we were little we remembered the bonfires stretching eight or nine meters high. Now they only reached a humble three or four. There were about twenty five to thirty bonfires then, and all we could think about now was how reckless we had been with what timber we had. We didn't think to ration it or stockpile through the seasons. The trees were dead so we used them all for the fear that they would not burn bright enough or long enough, that the tourists would sneak ashore and wreck our way of life.

Once our skeleton was done we noticed the cherry blossom sun was falling in the sky, its rose gold light dimming to dusk. Our pace was not quite urgent enough. Our bodies ached and our hands throbbed so sore we felt they could fall off at any moment.

We now had helpers holding our ladders stable as we fixed the timber flesh to our bonfire's skeleton from up high. We had helpers passing small bits of timber, branches and twigs which we nailed together to make the bonfire into a piecemeal tree. The ones which were too small and fragile to nail in place we got pieces of twine and tied them tight to the upper limbs.

It was almost full dark by the time we were finished fleshing out our bonfire. The other workers had finished and gathered to watch us finish this thing. Some of them pushed carts across the beach and stabbed unlit torches into the sand around the bonfires. These were the torches we would take home to heat our houses throughout the coming season.

When Margot and I were done we came down from our ladders and saw a parade of people coming down from town led by the mayor of the Isle of Flowers, carrying the one lit torch to set the bonfires alight.

The mayor's name was Carmel and she had bright red hair like she was born to carry fire, both in her heart and in her hands.

At last our work was done and we lay down on the beach with front row seats to watch the lighting ceremony bring about the end of Bonfire Day.

LOTUS FLOWERS

When the cherry blossom sun disappeared completely, the lotus flower moon glittered in the sky. It was pale blue and ice cold and it served as an ever-present reminder that we were living in the season of the Cold.

The mayor came down on the beach from the far side where the bonfires were distant. She lit her first bonfire to wild applause and marched her parade on to the next and the next until the beach lit up with a hot orange glow and crackled and popped as the wood begged the mercy of the flame.

She gave no such mercy.

As she approached our bonfire her face flickered the warm colours of the firelight, shadows forming sharp and dark upon the edges of her face. She lit the base of the bonfire and it quickly took to flame, consuming the heart and sending the heat radiating outwards, latching on to the bones and flesh, our piecemeal bonfire tree transforming the darkness to light.

Margot and I held each other in our arms and stared into the flames, mesmerised by the shape and colour.

Once the bonfires were all lit the parade circled back around upon the beach and gathered around the mayor. By now the flames were burning high, smoke rising to the heavens, swirling into the night sky. The mayor cleared her throat.

"And so the ocean swallows the light," she intoned.

"And so the Cold begins," we chanted back.

"May the bonfires burn throughout the Cold and keep our bodies safe from tourists," she said.

"May the bonfires ward them from our shores," we replied.

"May we cherish the trees who sacrificed their lives to protect us,"she said.

"May they grow tall and strong in the afterlife," we called out.

"And fuse their souls with the humans who lost their lives throughout the year." Her voice was strong, carrying loud and clear across the crowd.

"May they go safe and sound into the afterlife," we said.

We cheered our support for her, and then she disappeared into the gathered crowd as quick as a heartbeat, leaving us mesmerised by the building fires.

Members of the crowd came forward and picked up their household torches and dipped them into the hearts of the burning bonfires. The whole town filtered through as the night progressed and dissipated until there were few of us left.

Usually Margot and I were here with our families each year. We would get our torch and go. But this year we did our own thing. We watched the others come and go and drank in the beauty of the cool shimmering beauty of the lotus moon, and we noticed for the first time in all our years the parade which came with the mayor's torch, they had brought with them dozens of blue iceboxes and set them down around the bonfires and waited until the evening had quietened right down.

The iceboxes themselves were familiar, but we had never seen what was in them, why they were brought down to the beach every year. It seemed an odd tradition until we approached one of the ice boxes and saw for ourselves. The box was clear and made of plastic, a double layer of insulation which was lined with lotus flowers to keep the box and its contents cool. The flowers ranged in colour from a pale ice blue to a deep blue ocean and out into the spectrum of violets and purples, swimming with all those beautiful hues, with the flowers seeming to change colour while we watched, a hypnotic display like watching the waves crash and wash over your own feet.

On the box was a name, both familiar and distant. The people who carried the icebox down to the beach watched us warily like they were guarding some long lost treasure. Instead, we found that they were just guarding the refrigerated body of their deceased grandfather. Two young men, tears in their eyes, pried open the lid – we gave them space – and pulled out the body of a man who had died between the last Cold and now.

We followed them with our eyes from the icebox to the bonfire and they lifted him into the heart of the fire, piled and tumbled in with the others who had started to turn to ash already. All up and down the beach we saw that Bonfire Day had become a ritual of burning bodies in the night.

May we cherish the trees who sacrificed their lives to protect us and fuse their souls with the humans who lost their lives throughout the year.

We felt the sand grow cold beneath our feet as the ice cold lotus flowers began to worm their way up through the sand.

By morning they would coat the beach.

THE WATCHMEN

When Margot and I parted ways at the end of the night it was tough to let her go because her warmth was gone in an instant and the bitter chill drove straight into my bones. My house was only a few rows down from hers, but the street was dark and quiet and penetratingly cold. It felt like there were tourists hiding behind every shadow, casting shapes long and unusual about the town, forming smiles and laughter most unnatural.

Before I disappeared inside my home (where my family had already ignited their lanterns and heaters from the bonfires) I looked up at the lotus moon, truly beautiful, and its refracted light shimmering down on the mountainside, where once upon a time the trees ran all the way up the slope but now receded like a bald spot more than half way down. The cherry blossoms were dying much faster than they could grow, and I knew it was all because of the tourists invading our town.

In the morning the streets were lined with lotus flowers grown like weeds, settled in for the season. The sky was once again wrapped in the rose gold light of the cherry blossom sun, but now it was partnered with the lotus moon hanging still above the mountain, warping the rose gold into an ethereal violet/indigo bloom. The light became a fractal pattern around the moon, spiralling slowly on the spot while the sun rose to meet it, the colours melting in a constant state of change.

Breakfast was fried watermelon with a cup of boiling hot lotus flower tea. The tea was made so hot because otherwise it would become ice cold within minutes. While the heat from the tea was still inside me I walked down to the beach to check on the bonfires. This was a ritual that we would all make throughout the season to feed more wood into the fires and to make sure they were still effectively burning to keep the tourists at bay.

I stopped at Margot's house on the way and her mother, Barb, opened the door. She stood in the doorway, dressing gown and slippers on, eyes taking a moment to adjust to the sun.

"Blanko, hi," She said. "What are... what are you doing here so early?" She seemed a little dazed and confused.

It was mid-morning, not an unusual time for me to

pop in to see Margot.

"Sorry," I said. I don't quite know why I apologised. "Can I come in, please?"

"Margot's sick," she replied bluntly. "Caught a cold." Barb narrowed the door to close it.

"Can I at least see her, speak to her briefly?" She had seemed perfectly fine last night.

"No, she's sleeping. She needs her rest. Good day, Blanko. May the tourists never climb ashore," she said.

"May they never see the light of town," I replied. The door was already closed.

I stopped outside Margot's window and placed a palm on the glass. "Get well soon, Margot," I said. I thought I heard movement from within her room, and while my voice was just a whisper, I thought my words got through to her and gave her some level of comfort.

I continued on to the beach, where the bonfires were still blazing strong and the sand had been covered by a blanket of lotus flowers. They were ice cold to touch, so now everybody on the beach had thick boots on to prevent frostbite and heavy jackets to keep themselves from catching colds.

The townsfolk were already hard at work plucking flowers from around the base of the bonfires to keep them from getting too close and risk putting the fires out. They wore thick gloves to handle the flowers. Others brought timber from the stockpiles to add to the fires to keep them burning strong, careful to place each log and branch carefully so as not to waste it. Our reserves had to last us through the coming months. We couldn't sacrifice a piece of timber for a wasted burn.

I turned to Margot to comment on how beautiful it was to see the whole town coming together like this but I had forgotten that she was not here. Instead I grabbed some timber and loaded it into the bonfire that we built together, shifting some of the burning wood, causing it to pop and crackle, falling apart with a nudge from its sister branch.

Ash wafted up, a combination of burned plant-matter and human-matter. A column of heat rising to signal that the bonfire had accepted my offering.

Positioned all along the beach like stitches on the shore there were certain townsfolk sitting up high on watchtower seats, torches sitting in special made holders, binoculars slung around their necks and often puckered up to their eyes, scanning the ocean for tourists. Every moment of every day they kept their eyes on the ocean, rotating shifts throughout the day and night, always in a perpetual state of paranoia, sitting on the edge, often on the brink of slipping into a deep and dreamless sleep.

The watchmen, like the bonfires, had thinned over the years, and their hours grew longer, their fatigue stretching like toffee slow and gradual towards oblivion.

Their unease was compounded by the truth-seekers which gathered on the beach to highlight the impending threat of tourists, with many of the mad folk wildly convinced that we were beyond all hope and that there were more tourists here than townsfolk.

The mad folk believed that they were all who they said they were, but also that everybody else could be tourists in townsfolk bodies. They wore the bark of cherry blossom trees like armour and smelled like earth and rotten watermelons. They pointed at the watchmen and accused them of being tourists in disguise, having infiltrated our safeguard, they would let the tourists come right in undetected and overthrow the rest of us.

Their conspiracies stretched so far, and many details varied depending on who you spoke to, but each member referenced a kernel of truth, a connection here and there which knitted their logic together with a few wild stretches.

"Watch out for your friends and loved ones!" a mad man cried out to no one in particular. I watched him from a distance, lest he try to single me out for conversion or accusation. "Every single one of you here knows someone close to you, a relative or a friend, who is not who they say they are. The tourists have sunk their claws into this town far more than you can imagine!"

Few people gathered around him to hear what he had to say, but most went about their business tending the fires and plucking the flowers to stop and listen.

"Keep an eye out for the warning signs," he announced. "One: Loss of memory. They do not know precisely where they are or who they are. They will try to pass this off as a random lapse. They might *forget* something their actual self never would. Do not be fooled. Two!" He held up two fingers in the air dramatically. "Strange behaviours. Acting out of character. Suddenly craving foods you know they hate or going strange places and doing things they never normally do. Beware. Three: Hiding things from those they trust. Sneaking around when they're alone, making excuses to be alone, pretending to be sick to avoid confrontation. These people are no longer your friends! They are tourists! And you *know* what you need to do here, people! Take action. Drag their sorry selves out into the public and show the tourists that they can't hide from us. They can't blend in. They can't steal our lives without a fight. We need to hold each other accountable and we need to make sure we've got the right people in the watchtowers so we know that we don't have no more tourists threatening our way of life!"

He threw his arms up in frustration. The small crowd which had gathered around him made awkward glances at the watchman nearby.

"What's up, Petey," the watchman called down to him.

"Hey Yusef, don't go tourist on me man!" Petey called back.

I missed Margot. I thought about what Petey said about tourists pretending to be sick, acting strange, wanting to be alone. I knew Margot better than that, I knew she wouldn't have been overtaken by a tourists overnight. She couldn't have. And yet that seed of doubt was planted in the pit of my stomach as I left Petey with Yusef and wandered further along the beach.

THE TOURIST

Someone screamed from up the beach and people flocked to see what was going on.

People yelling "Tourist! Tourist!" into the air, causing a tension and panic to linger on the beach.

I knew there were a few tourists among us, going by unnoticed blending in with the rest of us, moving swift and silent like ghosts, and I had seen tourists caught and killed and burned from afar, but each time I had been on the beach when one arrived I had been under the watchful eyes of my parents who had always steered me clear of the violence, always cautious of me getting too close, ever cautious of their corrupting presence and potential for deep penetrating nightmares.

Now I was full grown I was old enough to process such images, to have such freedoms, to linger on the fringe and explore the danger zones of our culture, and I pushed my way through the gathered crowd on the beach, feeling pulled in by the tourist to witness the horror for myself.

It was magnetic. My legs did the walking automatic up to it, eyes drawn to the thing laying on the beach about which the crowd gathered.

It was a gloss black thing, roughly the size and shape of a human. Its limbs were webbed like fins, having just come out of the water, and its skin was dark like space on the warm moonless nights of the season of the Blossom, pockmarked with the rose gold stars of distant cherry blossom stars, the suns of distant galaxies, and the tinge of a beautiful aura which was sometimes a blue-green aqua, sometimes a deeper blue, closer to indigo or violet.

The tourist's skin held these colours and textures fresh from the water as it struggled with its body pinned flat on the beach, skewered with the sharpened stick from a cherry blossom tree branch.

The thing gasped and cried in agony, and yet its face was a featureless mask, sleek and smooth, and if we didn't know better we would think it were deaf and blind and dumb. No nose to smell, no mouth to speak. The cries came from deep within and the tourist tried to slink back into the shadows or slink back into the ocean, but it was pinned tight in place, bleeding and dying. No sympathy from the locals. Only fear for what could have been and disgust for the creature that it was.

It seemed to look up to me as it made a final heaving grasp, and it clutched a cold wet hand around my calf, sending a bizarre tingling sensation throughout my body, and as it died I watched its limbs relax and its flesh lighten, losing its sheen. Its face came into being, ears protruding with nose and chin and cheeks. Eye sockets sinking into its flesh and forming lids behind which dead eyes remained still. Its mouth popped open and revealed a set of razor sharp teeth like a shark's, made to frighten as much as they were made for tearing flesh.

Hair sprouted dark and thick upon its head and the result became a sickening familiarity, a perfect reflection of myself.

I looked down at my calf where the tourist had grabbed on to it and there was its mark, the slick black texture of its former skin, like a tattoo, the stain of its fingers a reminder of what could have been, and what still could be.

THE STAIN

That afternoon I sat in my bedroom, soaking my foot in scalding hot water. I tried to scrub it off and wash it off with all manner of cleaning products, but nothing washed the stain away. I hoped if the water was hot enough I could melt it off, but I was afraid I would cook my raw foot tender before that would happen. It was bright pink, burning so hot I felt a little guilty for all the flame I'd wasted to make the water this hot while the day is so cold.

Never mind the fact that I couldn't remove the tourist's mark, or that I couldn't share this harrowing experience with Margot, if she was still even human. I was afraid that now she would see my mark and think a tourist had taken my place.

I imagined what would have happened if that creature had my likeness and I ended up getting tossed in the fire.

Bile rose in my throat and I took my foot out of the water and wrapped it in a towel.

There came a gentle rapping at my window, and Margot's face appeared there, gesturing for me to open up and let her in.

I hesitated for just a moment before complying. As much as I didn't want to lose my relationship with Margot over some stupid mark on my ankle, she seemed anxious, like she really needed to talk.

In that moment I ran the scenario through my mind, what if she were a tourist, what that would mean for me. What harm could be done. Did they hunt in packs? Was I falling into a trap? I thought of the things the mad folk said on the beach, the strange behaviours, the warning signs. I tried to think of ways to determine a real Margot from an imposter. Paranoia was becoming a plague in this town, and what you may call strange behaviours, what may warrant suspicion over touristhood could just be a deep paranoia unsettling the brain and stirring chaos through every waking moment. I didn't think I was there yet.

I also found myself incapable of denying Margot when she looked so desperate and afraid.

If she were a tourist I might have died on this day. Instead she climbed through the window and wrapped her arms around me in a close, tight hug.

"Blanko, I'm so glad to see you," she said.

She didn't look or sound sick. She didn't feel cold.

"I missed you today," I said. "I stopped by to see you this morning but your mother said you were sick."

"That wasn't my mother," Margot replied bluntly. "A tourist has replaced her. She obviously doesn't want the word getting out. I had to sneak out and tell you. Blanko, please, you need to help me out here. I can't go back home alone."

I nodded my head and agreed to stay with her. My heart felt a little warmer with her by my side.

"There's something I need to let you know too," I said, knowing I couldn't keep the stain on my ankle hidden from her.

I unravelled the towel from around my leg and recounted what she had missed with the tourist that was caught and killed from on the beach. She stared at it in awe, much less afraid of it than I had imagined, and I felt more comforted by that fact. Like maybe it was harmless. Perhaps something just like a scar, an exciting story to share, and nothing more.

BARB

She was out in the street calling Margot's name, acting the part of the concerned parent.

The fucking nerve of that woman.

"So what do you want to do?" I asked.

Margot shrugged. "I don't know. I just can't believe this is happening to me."

I nodded. "How did you know she was a tourist?"

"You know, I always thought it would be harder to tell," she said. "But it was a dead giveaway. Her eyes were all glossed over, and I found her just lingering and staring at me. Now I think about it, she must have been trying to figure me out. When I asked her what the hell she was looking at, she apologised and walked away.

That's when I knew."

"Real Barb would have fired right back at you, with that attitude," I said.

"Wouldn't have been caught creeping like that, neither," she replied. "And that was just the tip of the iceberg. Once she knew I knew she wasn't my mother she just sort of fell off the deep end, sitting right outside my bedroom door, flicking through old photo albums and cycling her clothes through the closet forming outfit combinations which never would have made sense. Every time I opened my bedroom door to leave she ushered me back in and told me I was grounded for accusing her of being a tourist."

"Which she is," I said. "No point denying it."

"Which she is," Margot said. "I just want to know what she did with my mother."

I thought about the rumours which circulated through the town, about how the tourists killed the people they imitated and buried them out in the cherry blossom forest. It was an assumption which was so strongly held by so many of us townsfolk we just sort of took it as fact. The more I thought about it the more I wondered where the rumour had come from, whether I could recall a first hand account of someone witnessing a tourist a) killing one of us and b) burying the body out in the forest, or even c) skipping the first two and finding a body already killed and buried and connecting it to an imposter already having done a and b and pretending like nothing had happened at all.

Then I began to wonder about that confrontational moment, the act itself of killing the original. How strong are these creatures? How competent are they at killing? I thought about the scenario where the original could have killed the tourist. Would they too bury the body out in the forest to avoid casting suspicions upon themselves as to their own identity.

We truly lived in a world of shadows, and as much as we thought we knew that the townsfolk were killed by tourists, these rumours too were shadows. Nothing tangible to grasp.

If not dead and buried in the forest, where did the bodies go?

Could the original Barb still be alive somewhere unseen on the island?

Could the tourist reveal that information to us?

My thoughts became broken by a knock on the front door and that tourist voice imitating Margot's mother.

"Hi Georgia," Barb's voice came muted through the walls. "Is Margot here? She's been unwell and she's disappeared from her room and I'm ever so worried about her." Her voice turned to a whisper and we strained to listen. "She's been acting rather *strange* lately."

We listened intently for my mother's response.

"I haven't seen her today, but I'll check with Blanko. I'll be right back."

"Can I come in?"she pressed.

Margot shivered.

I held her quiet and felt the coldness puckered on her skin, tensioned in this moment.

A MOTHER'S INTUITION

Everything from this moment kind of all happened at once.

The words outside my bedroom became muffled, like our parents were talking underwater. Their footsteps were loud and heavy, reverberating in my skull. Every day I wondered if the people I saw in town were tourists now, if I should be wary of them. I knew there was a good chance I might have brushed shoulders with their kind and never known it.

Now I knew for sure there was this tourist woman coming for Margot, and by extension coming for me, the concept became far more terrifying.

"What do we do?" Margot whispered. She glanced nervously back towards the still-open window like it was now or never.

"I don't know," I whispered back.

"What the fuck do we do?" she stared into my eyes, her face mere freckles from my own.

I kissed her and said, "be silent," and gestured that she should slide underneath my bed to hide.

She nodded with eyes wide with fear and she disappeared into the pile of dirty clothes which had accumulated there over weeks.

My mother rapped her knuckles on my door and opened it swiftly. "Blanko, dear, Margot's mother has just popped in to see if you had seen her at all today?"

I sat on my bed, trying to act natural and hide Margot while lying and hiding the part of my leg which was tainted. I tried to look confused. Barb loomed ominously over my mother's shoulder, eyes scanning my room for peculiarities to prey on.

"Sorry Miss B," I said. "I haven't seen her since last night. I thought you said she was home sick, caught a cold?"

Barb sneered. "She was. But when I went to check on her the bedroom was empty. She must have sneaked out. Are you *sure* you haven't seen her?" Barb pressed, stepping into the room and examining the perimeter of the room, scanning for a place one might hide a daughter.

"Absolutely," I said. I didn't sound convinced for myself.

"I can't think where else she might have gone," Barb said. Her eyes latched on to the open window and narrowed to slits. "Why on earth is your window open?" She moved right up to it and poked her head out.

I took this moment to lock eyes with my own mother and indicate my uneasiness around Barb. "I... uh," I was stuck for excuses. "I just wanted some fresh air," I said feebly.

"Huh," Barb said, completely suspicious of my lies.

My mother had come right into my bedroom too now, and taking notice of my strange behaviour around Barb, saw the mark from the beach tourist's fingers on my calf. I focused my thoughts on communicating silently with my mother not to fuck this moment up as she knelt down and stared at the mark close up.

"What on earth happened to your leg?" she muttered.

As she spoke she noticed behind my leg beneath my bed those rose gold eyes staring back at her.

Margot's shadowed lips pressed shut and a finger held up to them in silence. She squirmed gently on her side and held both of her hands up with the fingertips of her left hand meeting with the palm of her right to form a 'T' for tourist. She pointed a thumb towards the feet belonging to tourist-Barb still standing by the window.

My mother looked back up at me and nodded.

"Accident at the beach," I replied.

I glanced over at Barb, with her hands balled up into fists, visibly shaken by the disappearance of Margot, eyes scanning the back yard for any sign of her.

"I know she was here, Blanko," Barb said, poison now dripping from her voice. "Where did she-"

My mother stood up and smashed my bedside lantern over Barb's head, knocking her out cold.

"Quick, Blanko, grab her feet," my mother said. "Margot, dear, grab the bundle of rope from the storage closet, if you would please."

HOW TO TIE A KNOT TO KEEP YOUR HOSTAGE SECURE

"What the hell!" I said.

Margot crawled out from under the bed to find Barb crumpled unconscious on the floor.

"And so the ocean swallows the light," my mother said.

She grabbed Barb by her hands and lifted her limp body up, indicating that I should help move her out of my room. I grabbed her legs, making sure not to touch her skin, just in case she could leave a stain just like the beach tourist. My mother's hands seemed to be unblemished though, so it looked like we were safe.

"The rope, dear," she said to Margot.

We lifted Barb and her head rolled sickly back on her neck. There was blood in her hair and on the floor from the smashed lantern. Margot darted out of the room and we followed her, careful not to tread on broken glass.

"I... I can't believe you," I said, still in awe of my mother's fearsome act.

"May the tourists never climb ashore," she said.

"May they never see the light of town," I replied.

We put Barb down in our living room and Margot came back with a large roll of rope in her arms. My mother rolled Barb over onto her stomach and pulled her hands together behind her back. She grabbed the rope off Margot and we watched her tie a simple, secure, tight knot around her wrists.

"Here," my mother held the remaining rope out for Margot to hold while she lifted Barb up onto her knees.

She got me to hold Barb steady while she took the rope back and wound it around her waist into a makeshift belt, then over her shoulders and through her legs, pulling it tight to constrict her movements. She tied it off at the back and tied a loop around the end of the remainder of the rope. A lead and handle with which to hold our tourist hostage secure.

She passed the loop of rope back to Margot and said, "don't let go."

Barb made a groaning noise and her head lifted up, eyelids fluttering open, eyes rolled forward from the back of her head.

Margot gripped the rope tight, fearful like she held the lead to some wild, hungry, predatory beast.

"You foolish woman," Barb snarled. "What have you done?"

She shuffled her body around, staring menacingly from my mother to Margot, to me. There was a wildness in her eyes like that of a trapped animal, ready to lash out at any moment.

"Hold tight," my mother reminded Margot.

"You've got the wrong woman," Barb said. "You've got this all wrong. I'm not the tourist here, Margot is." She shot her daughter a filthy look.

"That sounds like something a tourist would say," my mother snapped back.

"She was acting strange when I visited this morning, too," I added.

"Fuck you," she spat. "Believe me, you're making a huge mistake here."

She strained against her knots but they held tight and uncomfortable. Margot held the loop of rope tight in her hands, never breaking her eyesight from Barb. She watched Barb's face go from a pale white to a cherry blossom pink to a bonfire red with veins popping out on her forehead, to almost lotus flower violet as her constraints tightened the more she struggled, pulled on her chest and neck as she took short and sharp panicked breaths. Barb slackened on her ropes but Margot didn't once loosen her grip on them.

"What did you do with my real mother," Margot said softly.

Barb leaned forward as far as the rope would allow and coughed and retched and didn't offer up any more words of abuse or insight.

My mother got up and grabbed her seasonal jacket and travel lantern. "I need to go report this to the mayor," she said. "Sit tight while I'm gone, and stay safe. Tie her up out back if you have to. I'll be back soon."

"By the time you come back it'll be too late," Barb called out, but my mother was already out the door.

Margot put a boot into the back of Barb's knees, pushing her back to the ground. Tears welled in her eyes and started pouring down her cheeks.

"Why," Margot croaked. "Why are you such a horrible creature? Just tell me what you did with my mother." Her hands trembled and she wanted to just shove tourist-Barb to the ground and throttle the life out of her.

Instead she was stunned into silence as the corner of Barb's mouth twisted into a sly smile.

"Tell you?" she said, "Oh, poor dear, I can do better than that. Let me *show* you what I did with her."

TAKING THE TOURIST
FOR A WALK

I had a bad feeling about this.

My mother went out to get help and all we had to do was wait right there. We held all the control over Barb, all the power. We held the rope which bound her tight and kept her reigned in.

And yet she knew something that we didn't.

And knowledge is power.

And ignorance is not bliss. It's weakness. It's fragility. It's a nightmare of pain and suffering. It's a storm which sweeps you up and beats you around and leaves you battered on the ground.

Barb knew something I didn't. The problem was that

I wasn't completely certain what that something was.

Either she was the tourist Margot believed her to be (and to be honest, I was convinced at this point that she was, too), and she knew the truth about the real Barb, Margot's mother. In which case Margot would not wait around for my mother to come back and pass up the opportunity to go chasing the truth.

Or Barb was telling the truth (this was a stretch in my mind) and Margot was the tourist. In which case Margot would not wait around for my mother to come back and potentially blow her cover running the risk of exposure.

Barb and Margot stood at the open front door. Margot held the rope in one hand and a lantern in the other. She looked back at me, waiting expectantly for me to follow without hesitation.

"Are you coming or what?" she asked. "You can wait for your mum if you want, but I need to go right now."

I felt my palms sweating. Impossible theories compounding in my mind. *What if they're both tourists and they're leading me into a trap? What if neither of them are and this whole situation is a product of paranoia?* I shook my head. None of it was helping.

"Where are you going, exactly?" I asked.

Margot pulled the rope. "Hey tourist," she said. "Where are we going?"

"The cherry blossom forest," Barb muttered.

"There," she said. "Come find us when you're ready." She turned to walk out the door.

"Wait," I said. "How can we trust her?"

"You can't," Barb piped in. "But what other choice do you have?"

"I'll come with you," I said, feeling the uncertainty in my own voice. "I don't trust her alone with you."

I scrawled a note for my mother and left it on the dining table and followed Margot and Barb out the door.

The cherry blossom sun was almost over the horizon, and this time of day at this time of year meant that everyone was indoors trying to keep warm while the bonfires continued to burn bright on the coast. The sky was a dark violet with the lotus moon hanging there, ever present, ever still. We walked away from the distant glow of bonfires on the beach, down the street which led us up away from town to the other side of the island where the cherry blossom trees gathered and where we would gather as a community in the season of the Blossom to embrace the warm rose gold light through day and night, where we cherished the lives we had and paid tribute to the lives we'd lost.

We didn't see any burials take place, but we felt as though the trees grew healthier over here because they were nourished from the flesh and blood of our ancestors resting in the soil.

Coming here in the season of the Cold was a far cry from those memories. I couldn't stop shivering. Margot couldn't stop shivering. Even Barb, the inhuman creature that she was, couldn't stop shivering in the cold night air, lotus flowers blanketing the ground like weeds throughout the bone-dry forest.

I had my doubts that Barb would actually lead us here, using this location as a diversion so she could lure us somewhere we would less likely be found. But now we were here amongst the naked trees and the sharp-cutting shadows, I felt a little lost. I looked to Margot and she shook her head, confused as I was.

Of course, we dreaded the truth that tourist-Barb had buried Margot's actual mother somewhere amongst the trees here, but this was a new thing. A freshly dug grave would be obvious. The ground would be disturbed with a distinct lack of lotus flowers.

There was nothing.

THE SHADOW CREATURE

"What did you do with my mother?" Margot demanded. "Why did you bring us out here? Show us what you know."

She pushed Barb for a reaction. The rope was rubbing her skin raw.

"Okay!" she said. "Okay, ease up." She looked around the forest in the faint blue glow of night and seemed a little lost. "The thing is… I didn't do anything to your mother. Not directly. I didn't harm her or hold her hostage or anything. You've got to believe me." She tapped her foot and looked around nervously.

"What did you do?" Margot said.

She wandered forward slowly, leading us cautiously

through the cluster of trees. "You think you know what's best for yourselves. What's best for this island." She shook her head.

"What did you do?" Margot pressed.

"You think I'm some monster. A ruthless killer." Barb stopped where she was going and turned to face Margot. "You people are the ones who are paranoid. You're the ones with blood on your hands."

Margot stood there staring back at Barb for a moment, the silence cutting sharp as the cold. "Quit playing games," she whispered. "I don't have time for your bullshit. Just tell me what you did with my mother, whose life you *stole*, or else I'll push you off the nearest cliff."

"I can assure you," another voice carried down from the tangle of trees, a smooth, deep, dark voice, sliding invisible through the branches. "Your mother is alive and well, sweet child. This tourist made no lie in that. And too, if you wish to see her for yourself you must untie these barbaric binds which hold her at your mercy."

Margot and I searched through the trees for the source of the voice, but he appeared to be in a constant state of motion, a slippery creature hiding just outside our field of vision. Then we caught a glimpse of two rose gold orbs of light gently glowing in the dark, a warm hue of cherry blossoms climbing down from nearby branches to greet us. A creature most abstract with its tourist-like blackness to its skin, fragmented animalistic qualities to its shape.

This nameless creature with cherry blossom eyes (on an otherwise featureless face) lumbered towards us on hands and feet, bone white antlers jutting out of its head in an intimidating fashion. His voice carried forth from no place, the sound surrounded him as he walked.

A lump formed in my throat, as it must have done in Margot's, as no words formed from our mouths, no words even crystallized in our minds.

"A price must be paid," the creature said.

Margot let the rope fall from her hands and she walked up to Barb and began to rip at the knots holding her hostage. Tears welled in her eyes at the promises made, the thought of reunion which seemed too good to be true while at the same time filling her with a deep and heavy sense of dread.

The rope fell in the forest and Barb stretched her aching arms and rotated her shoulders to get the blood flowing through them again.

She reached out and touched the creature and said, "thank you." She turned to Margot and myself standing here in shock and awe and she said, "come."

We obeyed, following the light and warmth coming from the shadow creature. Occasionally he would blink and there would be a moment's darkness, and then his eyes would open back up like the sun or like the season of the Blossom.

We knew nothing of him except that he seemed to be more animal than human, and that he was perhaps the most beautiful creature we had seen. I held Margot's cold hand in my own and we kept real close to each other for warmth and safety. We tried to keep close to the shadow creature, to feel some of the warmth from his eyes but within that space was also an aura of uncertainty and doubt. After all, strip back the polite manner with which he approached us, and he's a creature who harbours and facilitates tourists and does... *something* with the original townsfolk to make them disappear.

I gripped Margot's hand tight. I felt her nails digging into my palm. I didn't want her to ever let me go. Already my mind was screaming that we should not have untied Barb. That we should not have been following so close, should not be trusting with what limited amount of trust we had left in this place.

Desperation makes people do irrational things. Backing out becomes harder to do.

I thought about my mother coming back home with the mayor being frantically dragged along, finding my pathetic note on the table, that feeling of defeat like she'd lost her son. The mayor could organise a search party if only to humour my mother, but Margot and I realised wandering through the cherry blossom forest, this part of the island is a lot larger than we had realised. A search party would be fruitless if Barb and the shadow creature decided that they didn't want us to be found.

Up ahead there was the mouth of a cave tucked away in a corner of the mountainside. If we weren't following anyone we never would have known this thing was here. By the passage Barb had led us along, we weren't sure even if Barb knew where it was on her own.

The creature beckoned us inside, where the light from his eyes brightened up the cave. He paused here with the light disappearing into a blackness of rock where no light reached.

"A price must be paid," he said.

Margot stared at the creature with his penetratingly bright cherry blossom eyes. "What price?" she asked. "I released your tourist friend already. Now where's my mother?"

"That was a non-negotiable term to your agreement to follow me here," he said. "All who enter this cave must pay the price. You, who wishes to be reunited with your mother," he focused his attention on Margot. She let go of my hand and met his gaze. "Come here."

She approached him slowly, cautiously, and he stood there still and stoic, casting the rose gold aura from his eyes onto the cool rock walls. He lowered his head and she reached out a hand to stroke his back like a good pet, but before we could comprehend what had happened, the shadow creature ducked his head down then thrust forward, impaling her eyes perfectly on his mighty horns, her screams echoing loud and wicked about the cave.

CHERRY BLOSSOM EYES

"What the fuck!" I yelled. "What the fuck!"

She fell backwards, blood pouring out of her eyes.

"What the fuck!"

Screams. Echoes of screams. Eyeballs on antlers.

"What the fuck!"

I ran forward and grabbed Margot to pull her up.

"Leave her be," the creature said. It lowered its antlers again as if threatening to charge. "Do you wish to join us?" he asked, head still lowered. The light of his eyes shone directly on the ground. Blood dripped from his antlers.

I knelt down beside Margot while she cried out. I could see the colour in her face give way to cold. The shock wore off and left the pain right there with her.

"It's going to be okay," I whispered. "It's going to be okay." I didn't really believe it myself, but I had to say something. I had to do something.

"Step back," the creature said. "I will not let harm come to her."

His words rang in my head a tone of comfort, but I glanced up at those antlers decorated with Margot's eyeballs and I felt nauseous.

"We'll get you home safe," I reassured her. "We'll get you healed up and then you can stay with my mother and I as long as you like."

I wasn't sure if she would last long enough to make it out of the cave, let alone find our way back out of the forest.

"No," she said weakly. "I came here to find out what happened to my mother. That's what I'm going to do."

"You're going to die if you stay," I said. "Don't die on me. Not like this."

"She will be fine," the creature said. "She had to pay the price, and now the price is paid. The healing will begin."

Margot pushed me away and pulled herself unsteadily to her feet. She reached her hands out to shuffle blindly further into the cave, following the voice of the creature she trusted more than me. His promises had captivated her, and I saw now that there was no escape for her.

"Smart girl, wise girl, you will meet your mother soon. You," he turned to me. "You must also pay the price if you choose to come join her, or you must leave."

"I'm sorry, Blanko," she said. "I need to know the truth."

I saw the pity worn on her blood-soaked face. I didn't know what else to say to her.

"I can't go back without my mother," she said. "I... can't do it."

She reached the creature now, and he stood up on his two hind legs and with his hands he rubbed a black substance into her eyes which stopped the bleeding and made her look like something out of a nightmare.

"I hope what you say is true, that you find your mother," I said. "I hope she is okay, and that you'll be okay and that you can come back to town."

"I'm sorry," she said.

The black pits of her eyes stared blindly in my direction. Then came a rose gold aura growing from within. Then two cherry blossoms burst from her sockets, radiating heat and light. Her face flushed with colour, her body stopped shivering. It looked as though the pain melted from her body in that moment. Her mouth twitched into a little smile.

"Everything will be okay," she said.

"I'll come back for you soon," I said, and turned to

leave the cave. "Goodbye, Margot."

As I came out into the forest I glanced back into the cave and saw two distant glowing cherry blossom eyes gazing blindly back through the cool crisp darkness.

PART TWO

SEASON OF THE BIRTH

The first memory I could recall of Margot was down on the beach on the first day of the season of the Birth. We were too young to know language and we were too young to know the answers to many of the mysteries of the Isle of Flowers.

At that young age however, we knew our rituals well enough. We knew that Birth was the shortest season. We knew that lotus flowers would pluck out of the ground so soft and smooth by the hundreds and thousands and we would toss them into the ocean so that the earth could feed the cherry blossom trees instead, and so that they could give birth to leaves and form little glowing buds which would blossom into flowers in the coming season.

We knew the ocean would be blanketed with all our lotus flowers, floating, pushing towards the horizon, glowing cool and dark, becoming darker as they died.

And we would celebrate surviving the cold.

And we would celebrate the bonfires which had burned throughout the season and kept us warm and safe.

And so we were young and innocent and gathered on the beach with all the other townsfolk, and we were too young to know what tourists were, but we knew they were things to be feared. We saw it in the eyes of our mothers and fathers that these tourist creatures weren't a myth or game.

I was cradled in my mother's arms, and you in yours, side by side while our fathers smothered us in hugs and kisses. Our eyes met briefly in a moment of slight embarrassment. We loved our fathers very much, but we didn't understand the big fuss, the incredible displays of affection.

We waved at them as they left us for their boats made from cherry blossom wood and their knives and spears made from sharpened steel. They would leave amongst the lotus flowers, out on the ocean where they would go hunting tourists, go for a day or two at a time, return for some rest, for the comforts of home, then go out again, out and back all season long, thinning the herd of tourists before the season of the Blossom hit and wrecked us all.

I remember my father telling me about the water-dwelling tourists being addicted to the lotus flowers, how those first couple of days were the most intense because they would see the tourists bobbing above the surface to snatch a flower before diving back down. Day and night, the tourists feeding, the townsfolk hunting. Blue flowers, black bodies, ocean blossoming with blood, the red smeared on their boats turning the pale wood pink.

That morning when our fathers left they never came back. It took us too long to realise what their absence meant, but for our mothers it was instant and it hit them like a ton of bricks.

Every night that season my mother would tuck me in to bed and kiss me on the forehead and say, "may you always remember your father's love." She would stroke my cheek and blow my lantern out and before she closed the door and sealed me in darkness she would say, "may you never forget his eternal sacrifice."

To which I replied, "good night."

THE PLACE BEYOND THE ISLAND

The season of the Birth was the shortest season, but it was the worst for our paranoia.

After our fathers disappeared Margot and I started hanging out a lot. Our mothers joined a support group to deal with their grief. They smiled less and their faces wrinkled more as they shared their sadness with their group while the rest of the time they remained cold and reserved. Emotion was a tight hug and a sharp peck on the forehead and a whisper that everything would be okay.

Our mothers became our sole protectors.

They gave us their strength.

They shed no tears in our presence.

We weren't allowed into their groups, so we often wandered down to the beach and watched the boats come and go. We knew not to hope for much but we walked up and down the coast hoping one day to see our fathers come home.

We were young and naïve, wishing for a foolish miracle.

And over the years we learned that we were one of the lucky ones, for our fathers to just vanish like they did. Sure we waited and hoped that one day, one year, they would find their way back home, but other families had to face the reality that life beyond the island took its toll on the tourist hunters. It took its toll on us all.

While they were out on the ocean, spending days on end with no contact but each other, nothing to do but scan the waters for tourists to kill, nothing to eat but dried fruit, it changed them.

We could see quite clearly the boats come back and the townsfolk disembarking with faces hung heavy and tired. While they should have been excited to come back home to see their families they were fatigued. The light faded from their eyes.

This was the worst aspect of the season of the Birth and the hunting trips. Kind and passive people came back exhausted and short-tempered. Their families began to wonder what happened while they were out on the ocean. And the only two explanations were that they had been attacked and killed and replaced by tourists and they weren't really themselves any more, or they had sacrificed so much for us and yet all their hunting and killing had poisoned their minds and turned them into terrible people.

Each possibility was a tough reality to face.

We could deal with the grief and loss of our fathers. We didn't have to entertain the idea of idolising the ones we used to love but had grown to hate. We didn't have to worry that our fathers had become monsters, one way or another.

We just grew older in each other's company while our mothers grew colder. We knew the suspicion that other children had towards their fathers, wives to their husbands. We saw the boats come and go and we observed the behaviours of the ones who came back from the place beyond the island, and we speculated whether they were still the same person as they were when they left or whether they had changed character or whether they had been replaced entirely.

It was something to pass the time while our mothers were in their support group, but it was not a game. No, never a game.

The feeling we had when we saw someone behaving nervous or erratic, behaving wildly out of character, we never knew discomfort quite like this. The thought of them going out again and bringing back another boat load of tourists. Bringing them into countless family homes, bringing them into our lives, hiding in plain sight, threatening the day they outnumber us enough to overthrow the townsfolk and reveal their true identities, their true flesh.

Often enough we would be on the beach and witness a boat arriving and the partners and children untrusting, sensing the odd behaviour common in tourists and those poisoned with severe paranoia. Instead of the warm embrace of a family reunion there were heated arguments over who was who. The accusation of touristhood was not made lightly, and the resulting downfall formed a tension and anxiety not just on the family, but all of us around them.

The families would be separated and an investigation would occur immediately.

This happened far too often for our comfort.

THE IDENTITY TRIALS

When someone was suspected of touristhood they became subjected to the identity trials.

Whenever Margot and I saw people getting dragged off from the beach we would follow them to the town hall where the identity trials took place.

In the town hall there was a raised stage with a raised platform at the far end of the hall. This is where the mayor sat in her tall polished cherry blossom wood throne and passed her judgements down on the townsfolk.

To her left was a timber birdcage structure in which the accused would stand trial. To the right was a barrier to keep the accusers at a distance. There were rows and rows of pews which filled the rest of the hall, facing the stage in order to witness the spectacle of the trials.

Margot and I liked to sit at the back and watch the trials unfold. We watched countless husbands and wives, parents and children becoming exposed right here for all to see. Every memory, every thought and feeling, every quirk, every familiar behaviour coming to light and marked down in terms of likelihood of falsehood or truth. Most cases were a brutal cross-examination. Harsh interrogations with multiple character witnesses, picking apart whether they thought you were just acting strange or whether you were not yourself at all any more.

The most interesting and intense cases involved the accused being given a clear verdict of townsfolkhood, then flipping on their accuser, knowing the one they love and trust most in the world would surely know them better than that, would not subject them to such torture and therefore must be a tourist themselves.

Fear and paranoia were a product of the season, and even once a trial was completed and a judgement was passed, we often felt like we knew less about these people than when we started. We could hardly tell if we agreed with their verdict or whether they had sentenced an innocent being to die or whether they were letting a tourist roam free.

It wouldn't have been the first time the mayor's judgements were called into question or her legitimacy as one of the townsfolk. All you could do in that position is deny, deny, deny.

ABANDONMENT ISSUES

"What were you thinking?" my mother screamed as I arrived home minus Margot and Barb. She had my note clutched in her hand, crumpled up like the fury on her face. "All you had to do was wait for me."

The mayor stood beside her, silently watching me approach with caution, watching me as I felt my guts churning, shredding at the thought of disappointing my mother in such a real and catastrophic way.

"Margot needed that tourist to help find her real mother," I said, feeling like my excuses would never land with my mother.

"Margot should have known better," she spat. "You should have known better." The weight of my mother's words were heavier than any open palm or fist could have been. "Her mother's dead. That tourist bitch is a liar and a killer, Blanko. You know that's what they do."

I nodded. I knew. I knew the stories. I knew the rumours. I had seen the accusations and trials. I had seen the creatures washed up on the beach. I felt the stain on my leg and knew the sort of things they were capable of.

And yet there was some small part of me which clutched on to some weird abstract version of hope. A part of me which believed in foolishly optimistic things like how tourists were capable of mercy and compassion and that our views on them were misguided. I didn't say this to my mother, as I felt like her disappointment in me couldn't get any lower. I saw in her eyes the blame of this act of defiance falling squarely on my shoulders.

I let Margot leave.

I let the tourist go.

I sentenced one to death and the other to go forth and thrive in the chaos and uncertainty.

"How can I trust you," my mother whispered, staring at me like a stranger, trying to figure me out. "I don't even know who you are any more."

"Mum. Don't," I said. I knew where this was going. "You know me. You *know* me." I stared right back at her. Tears were leaking out of me. My throat became tight, it became harder to speak, harder to breathe.

My mother turned to the mayor and said, "Carmel, I do not recognise this young man. He is not my son."

Tears now formed in her own eyes.

I had not seen her cry in years, and now she felt she couldn't trust her only son, felt she had lost the only people in her life she truly deeply loved. Whether she was right to make this call or wrong, now she was alone.

"No," I said. "No mum, no! You're making a mistake."

She stared back at me, then at Carmel. Carmel waited for her confirmation. She nodded. Carmel, bound by her mayoral duties, came forward, producing restraints from her coat pocket and latching them over my wrists behind my back.

"Blanko, you stand accused of touristhood and shall be subjected to the identity trials immediately. May your judgement ring true," she said, turning me back out towards the street.

"May the truth blossom open," my mother said, following us towards the town hall.

"What is happening?" I cried out. "How can you do this to me? Believe me, please! I'm not trying to deceive you!"

"Blanko, you are accused by your mother, Georgia. If found guilty you will be sentenced to death." Carmel's voice was cold and clinical. She had been through this process a thousand times before. Whether true or false, the process remained consistent. "May the light open up and cleanse us of our impurities."

"May the Isle of Flowers be purged of darkness," my mother recited.

HOW TO PROVE THE LIES
FROM THE TRUTH

The walk to the town hall was long and cold and numbing. Tears became frosted on my cheeks.

Memories flickered through my mind, of the bonfires, of the cherry blossom flowers, of my mother and father, of Barb and Margot, so much love and light in my life, and I felt it all growing cold, tainted by my mother's words, sown by the seeds of doubt.

I knew that if I survived the identity trial I could never trust my mother again.

Inside the town hall the mayor steered me up the steps to the heightened platform, steered me towards the birdcage lockup, closed me inside still with my restraints rubbing rough against my wrists. She instructed my mother to stay behind the barrier for the entirety of the trial and she took her seat up high in front of the empty town hall. Hers was the only authoritative voice which would pass judgement upon me.

"We come to order," the mayor said. "May the identity trial begin."

My mother was seated behind her barrier. I had to remain standing for the entire trial.

The mayor turned to my mother. "Georgia, when was the first time you suspected your son of touristhood."

She cleared her throat. "Just today," she said. "Right when he came home after setting another tourist free with one of our own."

"And for the record," the mayor said. "Who was this other tourist and who was the one they were with?"

"My long time friend and neighbour, Barb, was the tourist. Her daughter, Margot, was one of us. Margot will never be seen or heard from again."

"You don't know that!" I interjected.

"Silence," the mayor said. "Your time for rebuttal will come."

"And Barb," my mother continued, "should she return at all, should be subjected to immediate captivity and given her own identity trial."

"And how do you know this Barb is a tourist?" the mayor asked.

"Margot had noticed her strange behaviour and came to my son for help. Margot was hiding out with Blanko in my home when Barb arrived and I witnessed her strange behaviour for myself. We bound her and confronted her and she... didn't deny it," my mother said. "I came for you for Barb, and when we returned home the three of them were gone. I knew something wasn't quite right then, but when Blanko came home alone, I knew something wasn't right."

"Blanko," the mayor turned to me. "Does this sound correct so far?"

I nodded. "Yes, ma'am."

"So, Georgia," the mayor said. "Just to clarify, your son appeared to be himself when you left him with Barb the tourist and Margot the human, but he appeared different upon return?"

"That is correct," my mother said.

"And how do you know that he has been replaced with a tourist in this time frame?" the mayor pressed.

"It's... the only thing which makes sense," my mother said, as if speaking to herself, convincing herself of this version of reality.

The mayor turned to me and asked, "would you care to tell us what happened after your mother left, up until the time you came back home without Barb or Margot?"

I nodded. "Of course. It was Margot's idea to leave

the house with Barb. I was against the plan at first, but we had her tied up secure and never imagined things would get so far out of our control." My voice was a little shaky, a little uneven, but it levelled out as I got into the rhythm of my speech. "It was Margot's idea because she wasn't ready to face the idea that a tourist had killed her mother. I thought she was being foolish, unreasonable, but she was heartbroken. We had both lost our fathers at a young age, and now she was potentially facing the fact that she had lost her mother too. She needed to find out for sure. So I did what anyone else would do in this situation to support someone they loved. I helped her to seek out the truth, to know for certain that her mother was gone."

"And where did you go?" the mayor asked. "What did you find?"

"The tourist-Barb led us into the cherry blossom forest, where I thought she must have buried Margot's mother. But she was insisting that she was telling us the truth, that she didn't kill the real Barb, that she had something to show us, that it wasn't what we thought it would be." I took a deep breath. I was just waiting for the moment where the mayor would cut me off and accuse me of bullshitting so fantastically that she would immediately sentence me to death. I made eye contact with her and she appeared to be listening intently, drinking my words in with sincerity. I pressed on. "I know this is going to sound crazy and unbelievable, but I swear this is the truth. In the forest the three of us were approached by a different creature. It recognised Barb, but it didn't show hostility towards us. It walked on four legs and had the black skin of a tourist. It had antlers growing out of its head and it had cherry blossom eyes which shined a light for us to follow it towards a cave we'd never seen before."

"This *is* unbelievable," my mother cut in. "Ridiculous."

The mayor cut her a look which told her to hold her tongue. "Go on," she said to me.

I wasn't sure if she wholly believed me, but at least the fact that she was willing to hear me out filled me with hope. "The creature promised that Margot's mother was safe and that she could see her for herself, but we had to untie tourist-Barb and the creature took her eyes as payment in order to enter the cave. It offered me to join her, but I couldn't do it. I had to come back and let you all know. I still don't really know exactly what was going on or why... but I know what I saw and I know that Margot is in that cave with those creatures and I don't know what else is in there." I took another deep breath, making sure to keep unbroken eye contact with the mayor. "It's okay if you don't believe me. All I ask is that you don't pass judgement on me until you see for yourself. Bring as many people as you'd like. I'll show you the cave and you can make up your mind then. Please. Just give me this one chance."

The mayor stared back at me, then at my mother, and back again. "That is an incredible story, Blanko," she said. "I'm... not sure what to make of it. I've never heard anything like it in all my years performing identity trials."

I felt sweat trickle down my forehead, my skin began to itch. My legs began to shake restlessly and my fingers scratched my palms as my hands burned in their restraints.

"Don't you see what's happening here?" my mother said. "First, Barb lures these two children out to the forest so that more tourists can kill them and replace them, then she sends a tourist Blanko back to bring more. They're taking over! We can not buy into this bullshit!"

"Settle down, Georgia!" hissed the mayor. "Don't you think I've thought of that? The part that trips me up, however, is that the boy has gone to all this effort to come up with such a detailed and convincing story. Why have I never heard of this before? Why would a tourist put himself at risk of exposing himself like this in the first place, then go to such lengths to fabricate such a vivid story to explain it all?"

There was a moment of silence.

"Blanko, you shall have your second chance," she said.

I became weak with relief and fell to my knees.

"Thank you," I said with a heavy sigh. "Thank you."

My mother shot death glares at me.

"As a provision," the mayor said. "We will rally together all the townsfolk willing to join us. We will all be armed. Those of us remaining in town... shall be armed. Should you be a tourist after all of this, we will not be lured into your trap. Understood?"

"Understood," I replied.

"May we suspend this trial until further evidence is present," the mayor said.

THE FOREST PATH BY DAWN'S ROSE GOLD LIGHT

I was released from my cage, but I remained restrained until that time upon which I could be proven human. My arms were aching. My legs were weak. I remained by the mayor's side while she walked up and down the streets calling for aid the likes of which the Isle of Flowers had never seen before.

My mother remained close behind us, and I could feel her eyes permanently fixated on the back of my head, both convinced of her convictions and conflicted with the possibility (slim in her mind) that she may have been wrong. I could feel that doubt eating away at her, carving a chasm between her and her only son.

I wanted to repair it before the damage grew too great, but it was too soon, too fresh a wound to heal this fractured family.

We stopped at the town armoury where the mayor loaded up chests full of knives onto wooden carts for the townsfolk to bring with them and hand out as we made our way through the town. From each house we passed the mayor collected people and torches, forming an intimidating mob prepared for bloodshed. She took the time to explain our goal briefly to the ones who joined us, the risks involved, the stakes at hand. The ones who stayed behind were reminded to remain vigilant, lest the tourists make a move upon them.

Of course, our safety hinged upon the assumption that there were more of us than there were of the tourists. The assumption that there were few unknown tourists among us. I had the added comfort of knowing that my story was true, and that perhaps the tourists weren't as violent as we thought they were.

When we had enough people to form a mob big enough to burn the island down, the mayor held me close and led us all up the forest path as the rose gold light of dawn began to lick its way up over the horizon.

As we approached the forest, the more I began to doubt myself. What I had seen, what I had heard. How I had interpreted the events. I couldn't be sure whether I remembered everything correctly. I couldn't be certain that I could have trusted Barb or that strange horned creature, or even Margot, as her choices were guided by her need to know her mother was still alive. I could hear in my head, echoes of my mother's voice, and of the mayor, the talk of tourists luring us humans out like prey. It seemed so simple, so foolish, you'd think you'd not fall so easily into their trap. I thought I knew better. I thought I had convinced myself. Hell, the mayor was willing to hear me out, and yet... I couldn't help but doubt. I saw in my mind those two rose gold lights from Margot's cherry blossom eyes, that blind stare which was impossible to read.

We came into the forest where the leafless trees stood jagged and frightening, even by daylight. The mayor looked to me for direction, and I looked every which way from tree to tree, the trunks and branches all blending into a likeness indistinguishable from each other. No clear path to guide or markers, no direction but for a gut feeling. Remembering the night time, the cold, the crisp, the calling of the cave. Knowing it was out here somewhere helped me to remain hopeful that I would find a way.

"I know it's out here somewhere," I said to the mayor. "It was dark last time. We had no idea where we were going. We followed Barb out here. Can't have been far from here before that strange horned creature came along and showed us the rest of the way to the cave."

"Did you remember how you found your way back to town?" she asked, sounding like she was beginning to regret her decision to let me bring her out here. "Could you start from there and work your way backwards?"

I shook my head. "All I remember is that it was by the base of the mountain, kind of hidden in amongst the rocks."

"That will have to do," the mayor said. "Let's head on up there and spread out and see if we can find it then. For your sake and for the rest of us."

My stomach had been doing somersaults, but the mayor seemed to have calmed my nerves. Whatever truths lay hidden out here, I felt some level of comfort knowing that the mayor was determined to get to the bottom of it.

THE CAVE OF FLOWERS

The townsfolk carried out their search with great haste, sharing their mayor's enthusiasm for digging up the truth. I lingered with the mayor behind the rest of them, and while it wasn't long before cries of discovery rang through the mountainside, it certainly felt like seasons had passed and left me here with my fate hanging in limbo.

I had been half-expecting some foreign magic to have swallowed the cave up whole, sending us all searching for a place which didn't exist, harbouring their secrets and turning me into a prize scapegoat. The paranoia was real, and the self-doubt was at an all-time high. I was just waiting for the bottom of my world to open up and send me flying down into the abyss.

But they found the cave and we quickly gathered around it and we were all half mesmerised by what secrets we might find within, and we were half staring at a cave thinking it was probably just an ordinary cave.

There was a moment of quiet where we pressed in and waited for something magical to happen.

Nothing magical happened.

The mayor guided me through the crowd to the front, and with torch in hand she strode confidently into the darkness, leading me helplessly along beside her. My mother followed shortly behind, and then the rest of the crowd filtered in, bringing their torches and illuminating the cold grey walls with their flickering orange light. The aura from the torches didn't reach very far, so we stayed close together as a group, uncertain what we would find or how deep the cave went.

I caught a glimpse of my mother's face in the firelight as she stole an awkward glance at me, still unsure whether to believe me or to hold her reservations until she knew without the shadow of a doubt. There were no words of apology or sympathy parting from her lips. I followed the mayor and the mayor followed the light as it danced off the cave walls.

Our footsteps echoed and our collective breathing felt damp and heavy.

The orange torchlight reflected off the walls

something red, a splatter undoubtedly blood. I felt my fists clench as the townsfolk clenched their fists around their torches and knives.

My mind leapt to the image of Margot at the mouth of the cave, desperate to be reunited with her mother, the shadow creature having stabbed her eyes, my mind zoomed in on the gore in her sockets, the deep red which disappeared to black like her eyes were the mouth of a cave. Red stained her face, stained her rosy cheeks down to her dimpled chin, down her neck the red river ran. It stained the collar of her shirt, absorbing into it in the attempt to bleed its way far and wide. In this memory her eyes didn't blossom into flowers, they continued to bleed until her shirt was completely soaked in her blood. She fell to her knees and begged me to save her and when I asked how she said "I don't know." She cupped her head in her hands and her hands formed pools of blood which strained through them and overflowed onto her legs.

This memory was so vivid, so bright and real. And then the shadow creature stood behind her and sucked me out of this distorted vision and I saw him standing there in the cave before myself and the mayor and my mother and the rest of the townsfolk.

He exhaled a sharp breath like blowing out candles and all the torches went out, leaving us in the darkness with only the negative image of the absence of light burned into our eyes, that rapidly fading image of the shape of the cave now disappearing like a distant dream, like it never was, the image of the cave now completely gone.

WHERE THE SHADOWS LIE AWAKE AND WATCHING

In the darkness we felt our collective heartbeats perform a syncopated rhythm. We felt our frosted breath form clouds we couldn't see in front of our own faces.

We felt the otherworldly presence of the shadow creature. Its footsteps were both everywhere and nowhere at once. I looked around for the light of those cherry blossom eyes but saw nothing. I felt a lump form in my throat, how everything from the point where Margot had climbed in through my bedroom window had been a gamble. I weighed the odds subconsciously in my head and I trusted her. I followed her out here, and the moment I had the chance to follow her into the cave alone I got cold feet.

The doubts stacked up and I felt the weight of my mistakes. Retracing my steps, everything I could have pulled apart and pieced together differently, if only I had the hindsight, if only I could go back and change everything after the fact. That's what the darkness does to you. It plays with your mind, warps it, makes you doubt yourself. A hundred times over, compounding your second guesses into oblivion.

There was nothing to do now but to see what fate had in store for me. For all of us in this cave.

We knew we weren't alone here, but the question lingered, how many shadow creatures were there? I had only ever met the one, but the sound echoed and multiplied in the cave. There could have been only one or there could have been one thousand. We felt their breath and their movement and it didn't even feel real. We were deprived of our senses and we only had distorted versions of the truth.

At least I knew a little of what was in here, and still my heart beat hard and heavy. My mouth was dry. My eyes stung from straining to see the impossible. And I had already had a glimpse. The rest of the townsfolk were truly blind, a blank canvas in their minds could paint no picture of what I had seen before, what I had described loosely to them. As stressed and paranoid as I was, I felt as though their hearts must have been exploding from their chests. Sweat mixed with fear pouring from their skin in sheets. Knives gripped so tight their knuckles would have been so white from not letting the blood flow through their hands. Blood pounding in their heads, knowing monsters resided here.

Watching.

Waiting.

Owning the darkness like we never could.

The longer they waited our fear compounded, what started as one shadow creature multiplied, one thousand, one million, the breath from nowhere pressing in on us. The cave felt as big as a planet and as small as a broom closet at the same time.

This was a game to them. The waiting and waiting and waiting was all just a part of it. Ripping us out of our own world and distorting our minutes, hours, days.

Maybe the shadow creature was punishing me for turning them down and bringing a mob into their home.

It felt like so long, but it was only minutes that we spent trapped in the darkness.

The townsfolk murmured quietly to each other, trying to comfort each other and figure out who or what we were up against.

Then from the darkness the rose gold light of cherry blossom eyes opened like a kaleidoscope, a flood of light obliterating the darkness.

"Blanko," the creature said. "Have you returned to make your payment?"

THE STAIN AND THE SACRIFICE

The murmurs died down as the townsfolk fell into shock and awe in the presence of this mythical beast they could now see. It was without a doubt the same creature which greeted Margot and tourist-Barb and myself in the forest before.

"You," he turned to the mayor. "Unbind this young man at once."

She obeyed straight away, fumbling with the restraints, hands shaking in the presence of an authority higher than herself. The townsfolk, armed with their knives, lifted them threateningly at the shadow creature, knowing truly that their bravery was an act, and that any move on the shadow creature's part would only cause them to drop their blades and run. Such power could not be defeated by steel.

I rubbed and shook my aching arms, my bruised wrists, and I thought about the shadow creature's offer. I noticed the blood stained on the walls and on the ground and thought of the sensation of gouging my eyes out. So vividly I could feel Margot here, fine one moment, blind the next.

"Can I see Margot?" I asked.

The creature shook his head. "I need your eyes before I can reunite you with her," he replied.

I stepped forward. "Why?"

"I need to know I can trust you," he said, meeting my gaze. "I need to know you're willing to put your trust in me. That you're willing to make the necessary sacrifices for the ones you love."

He approached me and bowed his head down. I flinched as his antlers passed dangerously close to my face and he tore away at the material on my pants leg. I stumbled back and the townsfolk murmured and I glanced down at my stained leg and saw the mark had spread, the black hand print blossoming out and consuming my pale flesh as though I were becoming a tourist. It ran down my ankle and up to my knee. It wrapped around my leg, forming a strange pattern like the stain itself were a live colony of some sort, growing its way through my body.

This wasn't how it worked. We all knew it wasn't how this worked.

"What's happening to me?" I said, not exactly expecting an answer.

"You were touched by a tourist," he said. "This is your reminder of that connection. You have nothing to be afraid of." His cherry blossom eyes were so solemn and beautiful.

I leaned towards them. I glanced at my leg and touched the patterns on them. I gazed at my fingers, half-expecting them to turn black too, but they did not.

I turned to my mother and gave her a tight hug. I felt the hesitation in her delay to hug me back.

"I'm sorry I gave you reason to doubt me," I said. "And I'm sorry for what I'm about to do."

I peeled away from her as she stared in silence, trying to process my actions on top of the already unusual circumstances which had led us here. I wished my mother could understand that I wasn't an imposter trying to fool her into a trap. I wished she could see me and my actions as true and genuine. I wished she had enough courage to change her mind and follow me into this unknown abyss. I could feel Margot was waiting for me with her mother, anxiously waiting for me to join them. I could feel the hesitation on my mother's part, as I had felt it too when Margot had given up her eyes and disappeared into the cave. I could feel the doubt creeping across all the minds of all the townsfolk here in disbelief of such a space existing in their quiet little island.

I stepped forward and nodded my consent to the shadow creature to cut his horns into my head and bring me into the sacred world inside this cave.

PART THREE

SEASON OF THE BLOSSOM

This was the season of terror. The season of insomnia.

There weren't enough of us townsfolk to kill all the tourists in this season, nor enough fire to burn them all.

For every tourist we could kill, there would always already be another one here ready to take its place. It would either be an endless cycle or an acceptance of the inevitable. We became ever-watchful and hyper paranoid in this season.

The cherry blossom trees were in full bloom and the Isle of Flowers was illuminated all the time throughout the season. It became one painstakingly long day.

The tourists came up from the beaches and they took on

our image and we were all awake and watching each other close enough that we would see any tourist attempting to drag their original off to the woods for disposal.

We had a system in place for managing it. We had fresh fires built on the beach with branding irons sitting in them. We the townsfolk gathered by the beach to welcome the tourists for the season. The tourists came and took on human forms and were branded on their foreheads with a giant blistering 'T'. The pairs filtered back into the town until the last tourist of the last pair received their mark.

The fires went out and the branding irons hissed in the ocean as they were put there to cool down. We felt a watermelon-sized lump sitting in our chests as we made sure not to lose sight of our tourist twins. We didn't want any shady business happening in the season of the Blossom, essentially the season of the light.

We felt a constant monitoring, the eyes of the general public watching us, always watching us, and we always questioned whether the eyes were human our tourist.

We turned to look but the eyes were always gone. The bodies too.

We were living with ghosts. We felt our eyes grow heavy but the light was always there and we were always under watchful eyes, even if it were only just the mirror image of our own.

LIVING WITH TOURISTS

The season of the Blossom is completely unlike the rest of the year. Instead of spending our time watching out for tourists and suspecting people of being imitations, we spent our time in everlasting sunshine with our doppelgangers, trying to figure them out while they tried to figure us out.

Each year the season came around we saw the reflection of ourselves changing as we grew. These creatures only days old from the ocean becoming the product of our own years of growing and learning.

In the season of the Blossom, they were branded, and so they knew their place. They were never to attempt to take our place, never to try to rebrand a human as their own and play the confusion to their advantage.

They were not unkind, not disrespectful. There was always a caution in the air, always the threat of violence should the fragile balance of this season warp and buckle under the weight of all these tourists on our island.

It was a strange thing to watch fresh-born tourists take to mimicking human behaviours like this was their birthright. They transformed into human adults in a heartbeat and you couldn't pick the difference if they didn't have that damning 'T' burned into their foreheads.

Trust was a fragile thing.

We trusted that all of us unmarked humans were not tourists before the season's start, but we all knew that was a possibility. We still ran the identity trials throughout the season of the Blossom, but it became much more of a heated debate as the town hall became overcrowded with the mayor and the mayor's tourist squeezed into the one chair, the accused caged with their tourist twin, and as many townsfolk as could fit in the town hall would squeeze their way in simply because there was nothing better to occupy the endless Blossom day. The identity trials became shrouded in noise, as the voices were multiplied, the perspectives fragmented and more numerous than before.

Margot and I went to one of these Blossom trials but it quickly devolved into a yelling match, a wave of noise which drowned out all logic and common sense.

For this reason alone I think most people sought out these trials as a source of entertainment. It was a sick and twisted concept of fun I never quite understood. The accused human squashed in the cage held a look of confusion and terror. He was helpless in this circumstance, incapable of pleading a rational case, regardless of his guilt or innocence. Most of the time these cases ended without a verdict. The branded tourist was destroyed and the accused human was moved to a secure facility to await a retrial once the season of the Cold had come back around.

We never went back again as Margot found the noise to be too much. It gave her a headache which rang throughout the rest of the season, compounded by the fact that we had our tourist doppelgangers pressed close to us, invading our personal space. For myself, I didn't want to go back either, as the spectacle truly made me sick. I had imagined myself in that situation, knowing a common statistic that no one is ever proven innocent during the identity trials this season. They were either put to retrial or found guilty. Going to trial was a punishment in itself. In hindsight I was extremely relieved that my trial did not take place during the season of the Blossom. I was extremely relieved that my suspended trial would not come to a close. My trial would be the last.

I remembered that season where we watched our

one and only Blossom trial. It was new to us but it was a true awakening moment for our tourists. They adapted quickly to our way of life, but the town hall became an explosion of anarchy.

"What was that?" tourist-Blanko asked.

I shrugged. "Sometimes we don't know who's who," I said. "This is how we try to figure it out."

"But what difference does it make?" he asked. "We look the same, we act the same."

His eyes didn't blink. They were the perfect mirror image of my own.

"You come from the ocean. We come from the land," I said. "We need to take care of our own kind. You folk are dangerous. You could be anyone and we would never know."

This tourist version of myself was so intense. The noise from the trial still buzzed in my head, but now, as we sat outside the town with our feet in the warm water of a secluded lake in the forest, his voice resonated deep within me. His voice matched mine in pitch and tone, our conversation bouncing back and forth like I was talking with myself. It scared the shit out of me.

"We're not dangerous," tourist-Margot piped in.

I looked at her forehead to make sure which Margot was which. This became a habit every season of the Blossom, everyone you spoke to, you'd be looking for that 'T' or absence thereof. Instead of eye contact, conversations were held forehead to forehead. Even outside the season of the Blossom we had to focus on regaining that eye contact, regaining that trust, to know instinctually that we are who we are.

"Sure," I said. "You're not dangerous *now*. But you're dangerous when no one's watching. You're dangerous when no one knows you're around."

I thought about my father and Margot's father, gone but not forgotten.

"You've got space on this island to share," tourist-Margot said.

"We don't have the resources to spare," Margot replied offhandedly.

We knew all the answers to their questions because they had been drilled into us over the years. We knew they said the things they did to gain our trust, to win our favour. We knew they did what they did as one of their many deceptions and manipulations. They did it so that they could survive the season and remain on the island in our place. Each season of the Blossom held with it the threat that the tourists would rebel against us and overthrow our way of life entirely, but they were to soft and weak and fragile for that. They watched and waited, but they never took their chance to lash out against us.

I never quite understood why. The conversations we had were enough to make me uncomfortable. Why were they so kind and mild-mannered? Why were they so patient and understanding? They knew we would wipe them out at the end of the season and yet they allowed us to do so. It was like they were stringing us along for a long con, but we had no idea what it was. We weren't sure if they even knew that themselves.

Margot slid into the lake to escape the circular chatter compounding in her head. I followed. Although the water was warm, it was refreshing beneath the blistering cherry blossom sun. I popped my head up and Margot splashed water in my face. Behind us the two tourists jumped in, making waves of their own. I dived beneath the surface and snatched at Margot's waist, pulling her towards the middle of the lake. She squealed with laughter and the others splashed as they swam to keep up with us. They knew if someone found them hanging around without their humans they would be destroyed. They were never far behind.

Margot squirmed away and dunked my head beneath the water. The other two splashed and laughed and wrestled with us. I was dunked again and tossed around, and then I felt Margot's arms wrap around my waist. I wrapped my arms around her too and we leaned in to each other to share our first kiss, and then I saw the 'T' on her forehead.

I shoved her away and the splashing died down. The lake became still and quiet as I stared at tourist-Margot in shock and confusion. The real Margot floated nearby, staring at me. I turned to swim back to shore.

"Blanko, wait!" she called out. I didn't have to look to tell it was the real Margot, not the tourist who spoke.

How could I not have noticed? My mouth felt tainted. Chaos brewed in my head and I knew I was done with entertaining tourists for the season.

I loved Margot, but the season of the Blossom suddenly became the coldest season of all.

THE DISPOSAL MACHINE

The end of the season of the Blossom was marked by three things.

The falling of the cherry blossom flowers from the trees, marking the sign of the coming of the cold ahead.

The cherry blossom sun going down, marking the end of the insufferably long day of the Blossom.

The rounding up of the tourists to push them through the disposal machine, marking a clean up of the town so there would be room in our homes for which we would sleep.

These tourists, the marked ones, bore no value to us as fuel for our bonfires. There were too many of them that they would smother the fires. We would not have space enough to burn our own kind, to mourn our losses.

The disposal machine was the quickest and easiest way for us to manage our transition between seasons.

The whole town went up the mountain path, right up to the mountain's peak, bringing our tourists with us, up above the clouds where the trees no longer grew. Here the rose gold light of the cherry blossom sun was eternal. It danced upon the light fluffy clouds like they were a blanket of heaven. Here on the mountain's peak was where we made our offering, the disposal machine did the hard work of destroying tourists on our behalf.

The machine itself was polished chrome, a mirror-like object which looked almost invisible depending on where in particular you stood. It had a platform upon which the tourists would stand inside a cage and there were two levers. The first lever sent a series of needles, thin as half a hair, through the tourist's head into their brain, killing them instantly. The second lever let the platform bottom-out into a hole in the mountain which sent them flying down into the dark abyss.

The process started with the mayor sending her tourist flying first, then she remained to use the machine for the duration of the procession as the townsfolk came up the mountain with their tourists in tow and went down the other side empty-handed. Once the mayor's tourist was done, the children were ushered to the front to drop off their tourists and leave, so as not to witness the horrors of the killing of their own likeness.

During that season of the Blossom at the lake, when the season's end came along we were old enough to witness the death of our own tourists. The children came before us and we waited. Tourist-Blanko and tourist-Margot knew this was coming and yet we could see the uneasiness in their eyes, in the way they shifted their bodies awkwardly as we moved up the mountain.

When we reached the top our tourists and the others around us were visibly shaken. When we were younger we didn't know exactly what was going on. The tourists of our younger selves didn't really know either. Now we could understand the weight of it, and we knew our tourists were acting how we would have acted if we were in their position. But they were not us. They were monsters forcing their illusions upon us.

Tourist-Margot turned to me with tear filled eyes and wrapped her arms tight around me. "Don't let them do this to me," she cried out. "Please. I love you."

My cheeks burned red as I felt all eyes on me, judging me. Judging the intimacy of the situation.

I pushed her back, sending her tumbling to the ground. I looked at the mayor and pointed to Margot's tourist and said, "she's next."

The mayor nodded and two men came forward and

picked her up, kicking and screaming, and shoved her into the cage. The mayor pulled lever one, then lever two, then she was gone. It seemed like this sort of thing happened all too often.

Tourist-Blanko gave Margot and myself filthy looks as he stepped into the cage of his own will.

Margot and I hugged each other tight and said nothing as we walked back down the mountain. We hoped we would never again have another season quite like this.

CHERRY BLOSSOM MIND

My eyes are impaled by the horns of the shadow creature. Hot and sharp like knives, blood spilling out and over my face.

In my mind there could be no other outcome.

I could feel the shock and horror from the townsfolk, watching me partake in this madness, but they did not understand. They didn't see Margot as I saw her going through this transition as I did now. They didn't feel the way I felt, the love and hope consuming my mind at the prospect of reuniting with her.

I did not cry or scream. I did not whimper.

"I'm okay," I reassured the townsfolk, but I did not look at them. I did not want to shock them with the horror of my stabbed-out eye sockets.

I let the shadow creature work its magic on my eyes, wiping the blood from my face, wiping the black substance into my eyes which took the pain away and stopped the bleeding. It was cool and damp. It was darkness like I had never known. It felt as though I were buried deep under ground, the soil buried in my eyes.

I turned now towards the townsfolk, my eye sockets now healed, and I felt deep within my sockets the seeds of cherry blossoms splitting and shooting, I felt the warm buds forming and a rose gold aura lighting up in the sightlessness of my mind's eye. My cherry blossom eyes unfolded and radiated a warmth and light throughout my whole body. I felt the cool air around me, heard the voices murmuring to each other, trying to figure out what it was exactly that was happening to me.

I didn't know for certain myself, but I knew it wasn't the pain of murder I had grown to expect from such creatures in the shadows. I couldn't see the cave walls or the creatures within, but I felt their presence, and my sight became a rose gold realm in which I could see clearly the ones I loved most in this world.

Margot was here in spirit, with her mother and my own and... our fathers sailed back laughing and smiling like they had never even left, never aged a day over the years they had been gone.

"Come," the shadow creature said, and walked further into the cave.

I followed. The townsfolk watched us, stunned, as the light grew distant as we left them fading into the distance and the darkness.

"Blanko," a voice cried out. My mother's. "What have you done?"

"I don't know," I answered truthfully. "But I did it for Margot."

The cave grew silent for a moment as I listened for a response I was uncertain would ever come.

"I know," she replied.

"Don't be afraid. I forgive you," I said, although I wasn't sure if she could still hear me any more.

REAL BARB

Here in the depths of the cave there were all sorts of voices both familiar and not. I could feel the warmth from countless cherry blossom eyes filling the room with their light. I could feel the cooler bodies of the tourists, somewhat reptilian in their unaltered form (all the better to swim through the ocean), and I could feel more beings like the shadow creature, and I could picture them in my mind's eye even though I had never seen all of these other ones before.

As I took in the mass of secret bodies here I felt the wind knocked out of me as a pair of arms wrapped around my body and pressed her warm body against mine. The feel, the scent, impossible to forget.

"Margot!" I said. "I'm so glad you're safe."

"I was afraid you weren't coming back," she replied. "I thought I would have to come find you myself."

She held me tight and tender and I held her back.

"What is going on with these eyes?" I asked, noticing the Margot I saw in the rose gold light was different from the Margot which stood right in front of me now.

"Isn't it great?" Margot said.

I didn't quite know. It felt too warm and happy, like we were living in a dream world, like there was no point to us seeing these things other than to overload our minds with euphoria.

"Yeah, but what *is* it?" I asked, clarifying my confusion.

"Oh," she said. "The cherry blossom eyes show only that which is warm and beautiful in your mind. Your friends, your loved ones, your home."

"Is your mother here?" I said.

Margot grabbed my hand and squeezed tight. "Yes! It's everything I could have hoped for! Do you see her too?"

"Yeah, but is she physically *here*, as in... *in* this cave?" At this point I felt self-conscious that everyone around us was just hanging around listening to our conversation. Outside the echoes of our own voices it was eerily quiet for a space full of living creatures.

"Yeah, yeah, come, let me show you." She pulled at my arm and led me blindly through the cave, past various sight-and-sightless beings, and then we stopped and I could feel her mother's presence.

"Nice of you to join us, Blanko," Barb snapped.

I couldn't tell how much of her tone was sarcasm.

"Yes, nice of you to join us," Barb's voice repeated, her tourist twin chimed in with what felt like greater sincerity.

I knew that Barb-the-first was the human of the two, as I could feel the warmth of her presence, the cherry blossoms of her eyes radiating her humanity upon me.

The other was undoubtedly the tourist. The very same creature we tied up and followed out here in the first place. The one we had accused of killing the real Barb while the real Barb was already wearing her cherry blossom eyes here all along.

I wondered how long she had been here, and how this had happened in the first place. I reflected back on the moment when Margot sacrificed her eyes to find her mother, and more recently to my own sacrifice to find them both. What caused Barb to make that decision? Did she have that agency at all?

THE SECRET LIVES OF TOURISTS

"Do all the humans here have cherry blossom eyes?" I asked.

Barb replied quick and confident. "Yes."

"Why?" I pressed. "How could all of you make the same sacrifice?"

I had thought my own decision was so natural, so easy to make, and yet I felt the burden of it weighing down on me all the same. I felt a jarring sensation between the rose gold place in my mind's eye where my mother's face was glowing, and the face of the woman who was my flesh-and-blood mother inside the cold, dark cave, unsure whether she would ever see her son again. I could feel a circle forming in my mind, the image of my mother choosing her sacrifice to be with her son.

But I felt that this model was limited. That after her there would be no more of the townsfolk willing to pay the price to join us here, if she even made that sacrifice at all. Not unless every family had their sacrifices. Every family with a tourist watching, learning who to engage with first, who to leverage the right terms to make the right call to set their plans in motion.

These were the straws I clutched at blindly.

"You remember the season of the Blossom," Barb said. "You know the one I mean."

I did.

"With the lake," she said. "And the kiss."

"How did you know?" I asked.

"Margot told me. We have no need for secrets here," she replied.

My face burned red. "What does that have to do with this?" I asked.

"They know us better than we know ourselves," she said. "They understand our thoughts and feelings in ways we can't imagine. These cherry blossom eyes... they're a gift, not a curse. They lead us to the water, but we must choose to drink."

My mind swirled with these new pieces of information. I felt like I was swimming in a turbulent ocean, with this place, these people, coming at odds with the island I grew up, everything I knew and loved and accepted as true, now thrown into question.

They say the truth is a hard pill to swallow, but how could I know what was a truth and what was a lie. This place felt so warm and kind and true, and yet I couldn't not see the Isle of Flowers as a place of shadows and myths, an image mutated into its own self-image, as if the entire island itself were a tourist.

I sat down and I listened to what Margot and Barb had to say. They spoke like born-again tourists, and I wondered if I would become like them, if my mind would un-pretzel itself and see their point of view more clearly. I had my doubts, but I knew I couldn't have left Margot here a second time, at least not with some answers, none of which I had yet heard.

A giant shadow creature came up to us and I felt the warmth from his face blessing me with his gaze. I could feel the power of his movement, massive limbs on a strong body. With such strength, I wondered why he didn't just command us to stop hunting and killing tourists. We couldn't possibly deny such a beast our obedience.

"Twelve thousand years," his voice was coarse like the stones of this cave. His breaths were slow and heavy. "Twelve thousand years I have watched over this island, our children, these... tourists... as you call them. My kind have been here since the island was just a child, and the sun was just a little glowing seed in a sky black as the night, black as the children which climbed from our bodies and took to imitating every creature, every thing they could find. To learn, to grow, to become greater than their material selves. They left and grew and multiplied. They crossed the ocean back and forth and became far richer because of it."

I could picture his face, wise and old, dim light of his cherry blossom eyes drooping from his eyes some thousands of years old. He had no antlers. I knew. I could feel it. But I knew his face once black was now covered with moss and bark, like a beard which was slowly consuming his entire face.

"Then came the humans," he said, and I could hear the disdain in his voice.

FIRST CONTACT

"It was the middle of the season of the Cold, some couple of hundred years ago," the beastly shadow creature said. "The winds were wild, the lotus flower moon hung large and low. The ocean was swollen from hard and heavy rains. The waves were unforgiving. The night seemed like it would never end."

In my mind's eye I could picture it all crystal clear. It sent a shiver down my spine as his voice swam through my head, nestling right where I couldn't ignore it. I knew he had been there. I knew he had lived these moments as he passed the memories on to me.

"By morning the ocean had calmed. The rain was a sprinkle downgraded from its former torrential downpour. The light of the cherry blossom sun had come up and sent its glitter across the water. The beach was overgrown with lotus flowers blanketing it, as you are no doubt familiar. But after that storm there was the wreckage of a boat splintered on the shore, accompanied by dozens of humans who were lost and afraid and some were badly injured or dead.

"We greeted them with open arms," he continued, "but they feared us more than anything and set out making traps and weapons to keep us at bay. We never meant to hurt you humans, never meant any ill will, but we were given no choice but to retreat."

"And so you sent your children to watch over us," I said.

"And so our children became our eyes," he confirmed. "At first your people were somewhat receptive to our children as they took your image. The humans survived and then they thrived, and then they spread across the island and claimed it for their own. Greed..." He paused, taking in a long breath, what sounded like teeth rattling on stone. "Greed became the poison of your human minds."

I felt his eyes burning into me with judgement, like he could see that same poison within me as a thing to be purged, like he could wring my body and squeeze the poison out.

"The humans thought our children were nothing but identity thieves," he went on. "They accused us of lying, cheating, murdering. We could no longer trust your kind. Our children sacrificed themselves to be with you, to protect you and try to learn more about you. They tried to steer you towards a more sustainable future. Your town is dying. Your people still live in fear. You have no trust, no balance. Your bonfires will only burn so long. Our children brought you here, and here is our message: Change."

His message rang in my head as he lumbered away through the cave. Margot reached her hand out and squeezed mine.

"Come," Margot said, pulling me away like she knew exactly where she was going.

"What's the plan now?" I asked.

"These people, these creatures, they've been here a long, long time," she said. "Hiding in hope, waiting for the right time to bring balance back towards harmony."

"What does that mean for us?" I said. "And where are you taking me?"

"It's complicated," she said. "I just wanted to get away from everyone, so we could talk and think in private."

We sat down on the cold ground. Now that the echoes from our footsteps had died out I could feel the stillness in the air. There were a lot of people in this cave, but its tunnels led to places which were deep and dark and secret.

"Are we prisoners here?" I felt the need to know for sure.

"What?" Margot said. "Of course not. We're *welcomed* here. Can you imagine how we would be greeted back home? With our cherry blossom eyes and our insight into who and what the tourists actually are? We'd never even make it to trial."

I agreed. I understood her logic. It was all just coming at me so fast. It was so much to process.

"So," she said, with something more clearly on her mind. "Tell me what happened when you left me behind. How did your mother react when you came back without my tourist mother or me?"

My own mother's face flashed before my eyes. That lapse of recognition. "She took me for a tourist," I said. "She put me through the identity trials, and my innocence or guilt was dependant on bringing the mayor here."

She squeezed my hand. "I'm sorry you had to go through with that," she said. "So you came here with your mother and the mayor?"

"They brought half the damn town," I said. "They wanted to be prepared, should they find out I was setting them up for a trap." I paused for a moment, thinking about them gathered in the dark of the cave not far from the entrance. "Yeah, they probably still think it's a trap. I mean, they saw that shadow creature which met us the first time in the woods. They saw it take my eyes and everything."

Margot leaned in and kissed me. I felt a wave of warmth radiate through my body.

"Thanks for coming back for me," she said.

An eruption of screams echoed down the tunnel, breaking our moment up and bringing us back to our feet, returning to the heart of the cave where the chaos seemed to be coming from.

BY THE LIGHT OF CHERRY BLOSSOM EYES

The townsfolk had found their way in the dark into this part of the cave lit up by our collective cherry blossom eyes. Their knives flashed with rose gold light as they slashed through the air and cut into the tourists hiding here. The ones who looked like us and the ones who didn't. The madfolk had taken charge while the still-frightened ones amongst them kept their backs up against the wall and watched on with wide eyes as the terror unfolded before all of us.

The tourists and those of us humans with cherry blossom eyes fought back. With fists and feet, claws and knees and teeth, to rip the weapons from out the madfolks' hands.

The light of my mind's eye was flickering as people rushed about the cave, stabbed and crushed and gouged in desperation. Margot and I held each other's hands tight, nails digging into our palms. We felt our skin break.

Voices screaming. Words. Names. We listened intently to the chaos, attempting to filter one voice from the next. Somewhere in there we tried to make out the sounds of our mothers screaming.

Shadow creatures rushed through the cave. Some stabbed with immaculate antlers or horns. Some stomped or ripped or chomped. All were desperate to protect their children, and to protect us from our own kind. I couldn't find my mother's voice. As much as I had felt abandoned by her, I couldn't bear the thought of losing her.

Margot and I ran blind between the bodies, felt the brush of limbs around us.

A wave of helplessness consumed me and I struggled to breathe. I knew we couldn't stay here searching for our mothers with all these madfolk running wild.

I charged forward, leading Margot through the mess of blades and bodies, my mind's eye giving me directions, a map laid out in rose gold light, of footsteps laid out in front of us, breaking through the attack, through the tunnel, leaving the light of our cave behind for the darkness of the tunnel winding back to the forest.

I hoped my mother was wise enough not to follow the madfolks' lead. I hoped she knew better than to stick around. I hoped that both our mothers would be safe and sound. But regardless whether they survived or not, I felt like I had brought it all upon them by leading all these townsfolk here.

I felt their blood on my hands. I could taste it in my mouth. At the mouth of the cave I let go of Margot. I doubled over and vomited in the dirt.

ATONEMENT

We could hear footsteps coming from the cave, people following us. We couldn't tell if they were running away or if they were chasing after us. We didn't linger to find out. We took to running through the forest, lotus flowers crunching under our feet, leafless branches of cherry blossom trees snagging on our jackets and our pants. Rips which split the material and formed little red slits on our skin.

I had never had to breathe so hard in my life. I choked on my saliva and wiped my mouth on my sleeve, wiped the sweat from my forehead.

There were people back there dying and I brought on this conflict. Tears welled in my eyes, but I didn't care to wipe them away.

I didn't know where this forest path would lead us until we cleared the trees and felt the wind grabbing at our bodies, beckoning us towards the cliff.

"Blanko, dear," my mother said, sniffling through her own tears. "I'm sorry I ever doubted you."

She was sitting on the edge of the cliff, feet dangling over as the waves below crashed golden against the slick black rocks below.

"I'm sorry I brought you out here." I said. I sat down beside her. "I never should have let Barb and Margot leave."

"Bull shit," Margot chimed in. "This isn't on you, Blanko. I was never, *never* going to leave my mother's fate unanswered. You know that." She sat on my other side. "Besides, did you even pay attention to what they were on about back in the cave? It's all on the madfolk. Violence is their solution to anything they don't understand. You didn't force their hands. You were only acting out of compassion."

"That's my son," my mother said. "How could I not have seen you for who you are? How could I have been so blind?"

In that moment I wanted to tell my mother I forgave her. I understood. I wanted to tell her that I loved her, truly, as she had always loved me. But no words came.

My mind's eye opened up a rose gold image of my mother on this cliff in this moment, a knife clutched in her hands.

"I'm sorry," she said.

The knife slid into her left eye socket and then her right, mirroring the sacrifice which Margot and I had made to the shadow creature.

"No!" I cried out. I grabbed her by the wrist and ripped the knife from her hands. It spun endlessly into the ocean. "Margot, help!"

I tried to lift her up from the cliff's edge, to race her back into the cave, to the shadow creature's healing hands.

Her skin slipped through my fingers before I could pull her to her feet. She was gone in a splash, and my cherry blossom eyes fizzled with ocean bubbles from the weight of her body plunging in.

HOMECOMING

The shadow creatures spilled out of the cave with their tourist children following close behind. The humans with their cherry blossom eyes came out with them, with a number of them bearing freshly formed cherry blossoms on blood-stained faces. This was a new island, a new world we were all facing.

Margot and I joined them, and found her mother still alive and unharmed, if only a little shaken by the ordeal. The madfolk had their chance and blew it. The townsfolk had a new path to follow. No more tourists to hunt and kill.

They gathered around the mouth of the cave and mourned their losses, amongst them one of the shadow creatures, twelve thousand years of age, now gone. The giant beastly shadow creature smashed its fists against the rock, bringing the cave crashing down.

The mayor, now illuminated with her own pair of cherry blossom eyes, had told them about the townsfolk which remained behind. She had realised that we, as a town, as a community, had overstepped our boundaries and now we had paid the price. Now, all that was left was the hope of redemption.

We went down to the beach and tore down the bonfires. The tallest of the shadow creatures stood in their place, their light keeping us warm, letting the tourists of the ocean know it was safe to return back home.

"What do you want to do now?" Margot asked.

"This place no longer feels like home," I replied. "I don't really know what to expect any more."

"You know, I always wondered where our fathers disappeared to," Margot said. "I always wondered what was beyond the ocean."

"I like the sound of that," I said, as two fresh tourists crawled up on the beach and took our image. Two tourists to remind us of seasons passed. Two tourists to become our eyes and lead us towards our future.

S.T. Cartledge is a bizarro author and poet based in Perth, Western Australia. He writes surreal dreamscapes which blur genres and stretch the imagination. Logic and realism are his two worst enemies